We Listen...
...We Don't Interrupt

By Donna Luck
With illustrations by Juliet Doyle

THE GOLDEN RULES SERIES

Gino-Giraffe

was very, very excited.

He couldn't wait to get to school.

He had a very important message for all of his friends.

Most of all, he wanted to say it to Zelda-Zebra.

Zelda-Zebra
was his best friend

but

she was always in a hurry and she never stopped to
listen to everything that Gino had to say.

She would listen for a moment

and then ...

she would think of somewhere else
that she would rather be

and then ...

she would interrupt him and run off and play.

So,

of course

she would hear the beginning

but

not the end.

On **Monday,**
Gino-Giraffe turned up to school in his new, red,
bobbly hat.

"Hello, Zelda," he said.
"Would you ...?"

But
Zelda was impatient.
She had to go and play.
So she didn't let him finish
the thing he had to say.

Instead

she interrupted and said,

"Would I like to wear a red hat too?
Yes, but I'm doing handstands and it might
fall off."

9

Then she ran off and played until Miss Beanie
called them into class.

So she didn't find out what Gino's important
message was.

On **Tuesday,**
it was Gino's turn to go with Miss Beanie and do
some cooking.

So he said, "Would you like...?"

But
Zelda was impatient.
She had to go and play.
So she didn't let him finish
what he had to say.

Instead
She interrupted and said,

"Would I like to help you eat your biscuits? Yes, but
it's my turn next so I'll soon have some of my own."

Then she ran off to wash her hands.
So she didn't find out what Gino's important
message was.

On **Wednesday,**
Gino-Giraffe had art, which he didn't like because he
didn't know which colours to mix to make new ones.

When Zelda came over, he said,
"Would you like to ...?"

But
Zelda was impatient.
She had to go and play.
So she didn't let him finish
the thing he had to say.

Instead
she interrupted and said,

"Yes, I would like to have a flower just like that in
my garden."

So she didn't find out what Gino's important
message was.

On **Thursday,**
Gino and Zelda went to play football.
Gino remembered about his very important message
so he said,

"Zelda, would you like to come ...?"

But
Zelda was impatient.
She had to go and play.
So she didn't let him finish
what he had to say.

Instead
she interrupted and said,
"Would I like to come to the football match after
school? Yes, but I'll have to ask my Mum first."

Then she ran off to shoot a goal.

So... ... ...

On **Friday**

Gino was getting worried that he would never manage to tell Zelda his important message.

Everyone loved Fridays at school because Friday afternoon was Golden Time.

Gino decided to play with the new glittery play dough that Miss Beanie had bought.

Lots of his friends had chosen it too and he was having great fun with Millie-Monkey, Elsa-Elephant and Louis-Lion but Zelda was in a different group.

She had chosen to play at dressing up.

Just before it was tidy-away time, she came zooming up with a shiny red cape and a golden crown on her head and was having a great time pretending to be a queen.

Gino decided that this was his last chance. He stood right in front of Zelda and put his hands on his hips.

"Stop!" he said, loudly and clearly.

Zelda skidded to a smokey stop.

"Stop and listen, Zelda," said Gino.
"I have something VERY important to say to you."

Zelda looked very surprised but she stopped and listened.

Gino smiled at Zelda and then he said,

"Would you like to come to my birthday party tomorrow? Please, please say that you can. Everybody else has said yes."

Zelda wrinkled her nose, scrunched up her eyebrows and looked a little puzzled.

"Oh, Gino, I would love to come," she said. "But you didn't give me an invitation, did you?"

Gino shook his head and said,

"No. My juice bottle leaked all over the invitations

so

Mum said that I just had to ask everyone.

So

every day this week I have tried to make you listen,

but

you just kept on interrupting me

so

I was never able to finish the message."

Zelda-Zebra thought for a moment.

She thought about all the times that Gino-Giraffe has tried to tell her his very important message.

She thought about how she could so easily have missed his party.

She thought about how she had not been a good friend.

She decided that she would never forget a very important Golden Rule.

Do you know which Golden Rule she decided to remember?

On **Saturday**

Zelda-Zebra went to the birthday party.

All the children had a lovely time
and played pass-the-parcel and musical chairs and ate
red jelly and chocolate cake

and,

best of all,

Zelda took great care to listen

and

not interrupt

for almost

the whole afternoon.

THE GOLDEN RULES

We listen to people, we do not interrupt

We are honest, we do not cover up the truth

We are kind and helpful, we do not hurt other people's feelings

We are gentle, we do not hurt anybody

We try to work hard, we do not waste time

We look after property, we do not waste or damage things